BE WHO YOU ARE

TODD PARR

Megan Tingley Books

LITTLE, BROWN AND COMPANY

New York   Boston

Dear Reader,

When I was growing up in a small town in Wyoming, I felt like I didn't fit in. The other kids were interested in sports, but I wasn't. For my fourth-grade class photo, I wore a clip-on tie and purple sunglasses because I thought it was cool, but nobody else did. It was hard for me to learn to read and follow along in class. So, I was always trying to figure out how to fit in and be like everyone else. Finally, I realized it's easier and more fun to just BE WHO YOU ARE.

Love, Todd

Also by Todd Parr

A complete list of Todd's books and more information can be found at toddparr.com.

About This Book

The art for this book was created on a drawing tablet using an iMac, starting with bold black lines and dropping in color with Adobe Photoshop. This book was edited by Megan Tingley and Allison Moore and designed by Jen Keenan and Vikki Sheatsley. The text was set in Todd Parr's signature font. The production was supervised by Erika Schwartz, and the production editor was Marisa Finkelstein.

Be who you are.

Be old. Be young.

Be a different color.

Wear everything you need to be you.

Speak your language.

Learn in your own way.

Be proud of where you're from.

Be your own family.

Be brave.

Dance!

Play!

Discover!

Learn!

Read!

Share your feelings.

Happy

Mad

Sad

Silly

Scared

Proud

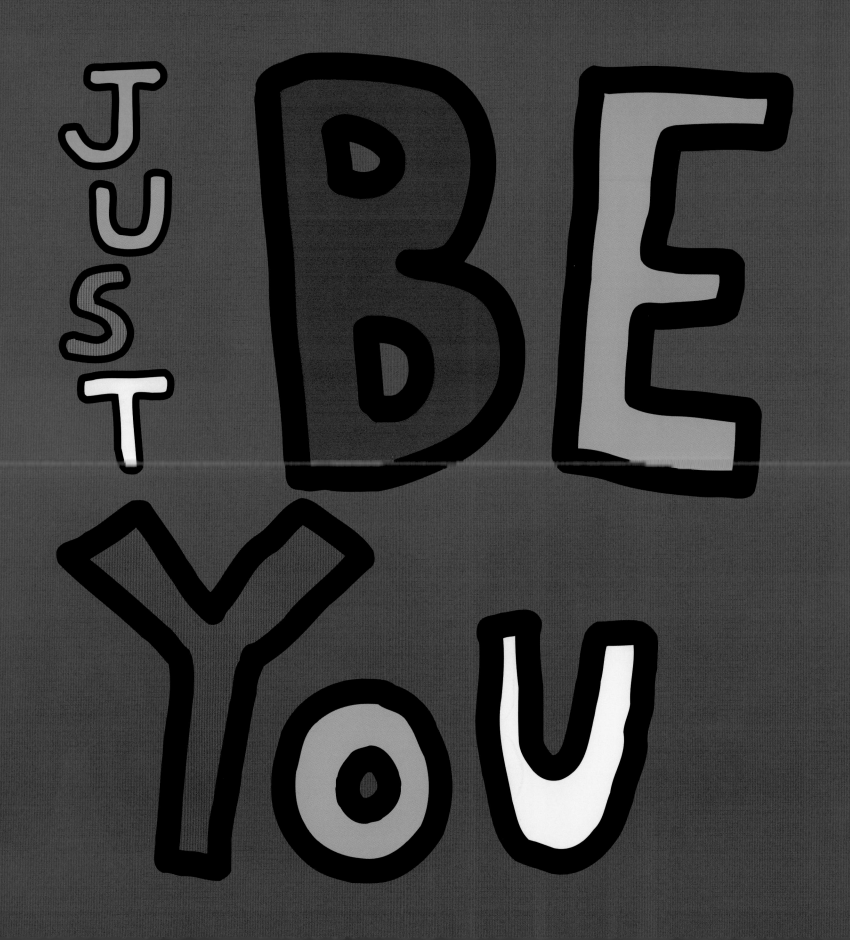

Try new things.

Be confident.

Stand up for yourself.

Be energetic.

Be peaceful.

Be the best that you can be.

It doesn't matter what color you are, where you are from, or who's in your family. Everyone needs to be loved. Always love yourself and BE WHO YOU ARE! The End. Love, Todd